AF484613

KANE CANYON RANCH

DENNIS H. WILLIAMS

Copyright © 2024 by Dennis H. Williams

All rights reserved. No part of this publication may be reproduced, stored in a retrieval system or transmitted, in any form, or by any means, electronic, mechanical, recorded, photocopied, or otherwise, without the prior written permission of both the copyright owner and the publisher, except by a reviewer who may quote brief passages in a review.

The scanning, uploading, and distribution of this book via the Internet or via any other means without the permission of the publisher is illegal and punishable by law. Please purchase only authorized electronic editions and do not participate in or encourage piracy of copywritten material.

This is a work of fiction. Names, characters, places and incidents either are a product of the author's imagination or are used fictitiously, and any resemblance to actual persons, living or dead, business establishments, events, or locales is purely coincidental.

This book may contain views, premises, depictions, and statements by the author that are not necessarily shared or endorsed by Outlaws Publishing.

For information contact: info@outlawspublishing.com
Cover Art by Eva Lee Williams
Cover design by Outlaws Publishing.
Published by Outlaws Publishing.
September 2024
10 9 8 7 6 5 4 3 2 1

Dedication:

Dedicated to Eva Lee Williams
Mother of Author Dennis H. Williams.

Award:

The story Kane Canyon was an award winner at the 2021
Wild Bunch Film Festival in Willcox AZ.

Chapter 1

Whit Wadsworth was struggling. With the outbreak of World War One, he had joined the army as a horseshoer. But a dose of Spanish flu had laid him low for almost a year. Finally, the doctors had discharged him on a medical discharge. Where he had been a strapping 180 pounds, he was now a staggering, stumbling 150. Upon his discharge, he had taken his mustering out pay and what he had saved and caught a train out of El Paso for Benson. Upon arriving there, he had found two gentle horses and outfitted them with a camp outfit and groceries. Then, working his way north along the San Pedro River, he had camped and rested, slowly gaining his strength. This had been his home ground growing up. He knew it well. Over the course of a month or so, he found himself on the banks of the Gila River just past where the San Pedro joined it. He was out of grub and almost out of cash. Now he was struggling. His horses were leg-weary, they weren't finding enough graze along the river. This morning, he made a pot of coffee and fried a small slab of bacon. He figured he had one more good meal and then he didn't know what he would do. Looking up into the Dripping Springs Mountains, a large gash of a canyon sliced it east to west. He was on the west end where it entered the Gila. He needed a job, but knew he wasn't strong enough to do a full day's work.

He knew there used to be a mining camp up that

canyon. Maybe if he couldn't get a job, maybe a free meal. He knew if he stayed here, he would starve for sure. He saddled up and packed up and started up that canyon. It wasn't steep at first and his poor worn-out horses didn't have to work very hard. The farther he went, it did turn steeper and the grass was more plentiful.

Late that afternoon, he found a spring by an old mine tunnel with a good patch of grass. Here, he camped, letting his horses graze on a good stand of grass. As he was putting his camp together, he noticed a buck deer slip up to the spring. He had two bullets left in his 30.30. He used one to down the deer. That night, he feasted on fresh venison. The first fresh meat in five days. He stayed in this camp for another day, letting the horses fill up and eating the venison every time his belly growled. At the end of the next day, the graze for the horses was short and he had just a little meat left. That morning, he rigged out and started again to the east. Late that afternoon, he topped out of the canyon into a basin on the top of the mountain. In front of it lay a vast expanse of grass with cattle dotting it. He rode on, hoping to find the ranch and a bed and a meal. The basin tipped downhill to the east. Below him, a mile or so, stood a house and barn with corrals. The house had a gallery around three sides. A tendril of smoke drifted from a stovepipe in the roof. As he rode closer, he could make out someone standing on the gallery watching him.

As he got closer, it was clear it was a woman. A

denim shirt over a pair of split riding skirts. They fell to the top of shop-made calfskin boots. The woman's hair had been a honey blonde, but was now showing a little gray, at middle age she still held a fair figure and a face with no wrinkles. But above all that, Whit was worried for strapped around her waist was a pistol. It looked well used, a lump came to his throat as he approached. He fairly needed a meal and a place to sleep, but this ranch woman looked hard as nails. He stopped twenty feet from the house and removed his hat. "Good afternoon Ma'am, is your man about?"

"No, I don't have a man. Not anymore, he's buried over in Globe. This is my ranch. What can I do for you? "She wasn't unpleasant, but still had a firm tone to her.

"I'm just out of the army, looking for a job. I've come a fair piece. Would ya have anything a man could do for a meal?" Whit was leaning on his saddle horn while he spoke.

The woman looked him over. The poor wore out horses, the light pack outfit, and the skin and bone man who addressed her. "There's hay and grain in the barn. Put your horses away. There's a bedroom in the barn, put your stuff there for the night. When you get done, I'll have something to eat on the table. "She spun on her heel and went into the house, closing the door behind her.

Whit found the barn clean and well stocked with hay and grain. He put his horses in a corral and loaded the feed trough for them. In one corner of the barn was a room. It was clean, had a cot in a corner, and a lantern on a table. He put his gear in a corner and went out to wash up at a pipe that ran full time with spring water. Cold and refreshing when he washed his face. Drying himself with his bandana, he started up to the house.

As he stepped up on the porch, the door opened and she stood there, her hand on her hip, inches from that hand-worn pistol. She looked him up and down with hard, calculating eyes. "I'll have to feed you for a week to get you stout enough to do a day's work. But you're the first man to come by in months. Come on in."

The kitchen table was set with steak and potatoes with squash and gravy slopped on to everything. As he sat down, she poured him a cup of coffee. Looking up at the cedar vegas in the ceiling, he could see they had been burned with the ranch's brand, a heart with a P in the center.

As he finished the meal, she looked him hard in the eye. "My name is Mrs. Boot. I'm a widow, and I know how to take care of myself. My horses come in every morning; be sure they're fed before breakfast. Stay at the barn until I call you for breakfast."

Chapter 2

Day 2

As Whit lay in his bed that night; his hands behind his head, he was thinking of the good meal and wondering what he would have to do to earn another one. On his way in that day, he saw lots of cows with unbranded calves. He wasn't sure if he could flank a calf; he was so weak. But if branding calves was the job, then he would do it. The boss wasn't much over five foot two or three. She wasn't going to flank any calves. Something about her bothered him, while an attractive woman, she was hard as nails. There was something familiar about her. He just couldn't remember. The next morning, he fed his horses and grained her remuda, when they came into the corral. They were fat and of good quality. Better than most ranch horses he had seen. Everything about this set up was first class, well maintained.

As he leaned on the fence, watching the horses eat, he heard a bell ring. Turning, he saw Mrs. Boot standing on the porch waving at him. He headed to the house, his stomach rumbling. Later, while he finished his second cup of coffee, his belly swollen with a breakfast you only get in town, she laid a yellow newspaper in front of him, the pages folded back to an article and picture of a pretty young woman. The head line proclaimed her the woman bandit stage coach robber. Whit sipped the coffee as he read the paper. When finished, she looked him square in the eye. "You have a problem working for a woman convict and criminal?"

After a minute of thought Whit replied, "not if you don't have a problem nursing an invalid back into shape. What happened twenty years ago is over and done with. It makes no difference to me if your name is Pearl Boot or Pearl Hart, I just hope you don't get tired of me with my boots under your table."

"You got a week to mend enough before you go to work. Oh, I sleep with this pistol under my pillow." She grinned at him for the first time.

"That's a good place for it. I never been shot at and I don't aim to start now." Whit smiled back.

"Mister Whit, you got a job. I'll call ya for lunch. Get on the mend." Pearl picked up his dish and turned to the sink.

On his way to the barn, Whit thought about his luck and what he had fallen into. "Maybe I found myself a home for a while."

Chapter 3

Cleaning House

Whit's bedroll was starting to have an odor that wasn't pleasant. He had bought the quilts from a lady in Benson and hadn't ever aired them out. This looked to be a good time to do it. When he got out of it, he tore the bed apart, taking the quilts outside and spreading them on the corral fence. He hoped the good clean air would take that rank smell away. As he turned to go back into his room, Pearl was standing there. "That's a good idea. I could smell them all the way to the house." She smiled.

"It was getting pretty bad. I figured today would be good for it." Whit was a bit embarrassed.

"When the horses come into grain, catch the matched Cleveland bays. They're my harness team. I need to go to Globe for some supplies. I'll be gone for three days or so. Will you be okay that long? Keep an eye on things around here?" Pearl was smiling at him again.

"I'll get by, I suppose, anything, in particular, you want to be done? I'm feeling much better lately, from all that good cooking." Whit hitched up his pants when he was speaking.

"You still look like a winter kill scarecrow, but if you feel like it tomorrow, saddle a horse and make a circle in the basin and check the cows. You can cook up at the house, but be sure you clean it up when you're done."

Pearl turned and walked back to the house. "Breakfast in a bit."

Whit poured grain out for the horses as they came into the corral. He had been eyeing the bays for a couple of days. But since she was driving them, he picked out a red roan for the next day's ride.

After breakfast, he hitched the team to her Studebaker wagon. She climbed into the seat and took the reins; she smiled down at him. "Keep an eye out for those Clem boys from the Battle Axe Ranch down on the river. They will show up here looking for strays once in a while. The old man, Mac, wants more from me than strays though. Keep yourself heeled." gripping the reins, she started the bays down the wagon trail east without a backward glance.

Whit turned and went into the barn, picked up a broom, and started sweeping his room. After a few minutes, he leaned the broom against the wall and stepped back outside for a breath of air. There, in the middle of the yard, stood an Indian, holding the reins to a worn out pony with an old man sitting on the pony. His rifle was inside the barn and he was too far away.

Chapter 4

Indians

Whit stood there thunderstruck. He had no idea where these two had come from. The man on the ground had a pistol strapped on his hip as well as a rifle in hand. The old man on the pony was very old. His hair all gray, his face deeply wrinkled. Their clothes, while shabby, were of the type Apaches wore with knee-high moccasins. The tall Indian held his right hand up palm facing Whit and said one word, "agua."

Nodding, Whit pointed to the pipe, free-flowing fresh spring water into the water trough.

As the Indian led the worn-out pony to the trough Whit noticed he wasn't very young either. His hair was shot with strands of gray and he walked with a limp. Whit understood some Spanish, so asked if the two would like coffee, to which they nodded a yes answer. When the coffee was gone, Whit asked where they were going, which the younger replied they were going to San Carlos. The old man was wanting to visit family there before he passed on. He then asked if he could buy a horse, his had collapsed on the journey. They lived in the Sierra Madre Mountains of Mexico. It had been a hard trip.

Whit told them the horses here weren't his to sell, but he owned one they could take. His packhorse was in the corral. He had regained his strength, but was still on the poor side. The Indian agreed to take the horse. No more was said about paying for the animal, but Whit hadn't paid much for the horse and figured if these Apaches needed the animal and would leave, it would be a good trade-off. The old man remounted the worn out pony, the younger on Whit's packhorse, as they turned to ride away Whit asked the name of the younger man.

"Muchacho," he answered as they rode away.

Whit shook his head and started to pick up the coffee cups and pot. There, beside one cup, was a small leather bag. In it were four gold nuggets. "I'll be damned" was all Whit said. He looked down the trail, but the two were out of sight. He pocketed the bag and headed to the house to clean up Pearl's kitchen.

Chapter 5

Home

Pearl cracked a sharp whip over the backs of the Cleveland Bay team and kept them at a trot toward home. She was four days gone from the ranch and for some reason had an uneasy feeling about it. The wagon was loaded with supplies. Enough to last six months or so, but something bothered her. As she topped a low rise in the trail and the ranch came into view, she could see three horsemen lined up facing the barn.

Whit stood between them and the barn. He held a bridle in his right hand while he stood close to the gate to the corral. Pearl eased the team down to a walk as they approached the house. Nobody seemed to notice her, as she reached the house, she pulled the brake on the Studebaker wagon and wrapped the lines around the brake handle. It was still a hundred yards to the barn. Stepping down from the wagon, she pulled a 12 gauge coach gun from beneath the seat.

At the barn, she could hear the big man on the black horse talking. "I run the last two hired hands away from here. They were a little sturdier-looking than you Mister. Pearl doesn't need any man around here. I'll take care of her and this outfit myself." He kicked his right foot from the stirrup and raised his leg to dismount.

Pearl had walked up to within twenty feet of him

with the shotgun pointed right at his butt. "Go ahead Mac, get down, but when you do, your ass is gonna be full of buckshot. I told you not to come back here."

Mac Clem had stepped halfway out of the saddle, but eased back into it. He and the other two riders turned their heads slowly to look at Pearl. Taking advantage of that, Whit had reached for his rifle, that was leaning against the fence. Mac and his boys were now sandwiched between two armed people on the ground. "Mac, you're not gonna run anybody off from here. You turn them horses toward home and don't let your shirttails hit your butt 'til you get there. You come back here one more time and I'll bury you here. Do you understand that?" Pearl had thumbed the hammers back on the coach gun just to emphasize her point. Without a word, the three riders turned and trotted off toward Kane canyon. Pearl watched them ride out of sight, then turned to Whit. "Let's unload the wagon and put the horses away. I'm tired."

Chapter 6

The Report

While Whit was unloading the wagon, he was telling Pearl about the things he did while she was gone. As he was talking, she was getting the stove going to fix an early evening meal. Whit had made a number of trips back and forth into the house with supplies. As he walked by talking, Pearl was absently nodding her head as he talked.

When he came to the part about the Indians, she dropped the skillet on the stove and turned to him. "What Indians?" she asked.

"The two that stopped here on their way to San Carlos," Whit replied. When he explained about the old man and the worn-out horse they had, she seemed concerned. Her eyes narrowed and a hard look came on her face. "You gave them water and coffee?" She asked.

"Yeah, then I let them have old Bloucher, my packhorse. He wasn't much good and I figured he would get them gone quicker. Look here," he pulled the little bag out of his pocket with the four nuggets. "He left these here, I guess, in payment."

Pearl took the little bag and opened it. The nuggets weren't very big, but any one of them would have paid for the horse. "They haven't come back by?" She asked.

"Nope, haven't seen hide or hair of either one, why?" Whit was concerned now, "I do something wrong?"

"Did they tell you their names?" Pearl was holding the nuggets.

"The old man no, but the younger one said they called him Muchacho." Now Whit was getting worried.

"Do you know what Muchacho means?"

"Yeah, it's a little boy, he wasn't a boy, maybe 60 or so, hard to tell," Whit explained.

"Little boy, what do gringos call a little boy, kid right? I bet that was the Apache Kid." Pearl seemed worried.

"Ah hell, he was killed a long time ago Pearl, couldn't have been him. He wasn't mean or anything, just needed a little help." Whit tried to explain.

"They never found a body when they said they killed him. I've heard he was living with those bronco Apaches in Mexico, in the Sierra Madre's. I'm probably making a mountain out of a molehill. You did right." Pearl relaxed and went back to her stove after handing the nuggets back to Whit.

After turning the team loose, Whit went back into the house and had a good meal with Pearl. He was gaining a little weight and was getting stronger by the day. "We will make a circle tomorrow and look at the cattle. Maybe start branding when you feel like it." Pearl was smiling across the table at Whit. "I'm ready any day. Maybe not do them all at once, but a few every day, I think I can handle it." Whit kept forking food into his mouth while he talked.

"You're going to choke if you don't slow down Whit, I'm not going take it away from you." Pearl was laughing.

Chapter 7

Workin'

For two weeks, Pearl and Whit rode daily. When they could, they would hold up a bunch of cows and while Pearl rode around them and held them together, Whit would rope and tie down three or four calves and brand them. When he got winded, he would rest and maybe chew on a piece of jerky. The days got longer and Whit got stronger, they were getting a lot more done. It seemed the more they worked out the better he got. He still wasn't filling out the skeleton, but he was getting physically stronger.

Pearl had taken a closer look at him and was liking what she saw. She always packed a lunch for them when they left the house. Whit still ate like a starved coyote. Pearl was always amazed at the way he put food away. One day she asked him, "how old are you Whit?"

He looked up from his sandwich and said, "I'm 45, why?"

"Well, I'm 48. We aren't doing too bad for an ex-con and chronic, are we?" She was laughing as she looked up to see a horseman coming across the pasture a mile away. "We're going to have company Whit." She said, not taking her eyes from the rider. "He sets a horse like Mac Clem."

Whit sat up and was pulling the short branding iron

from the fire. Laying it aside to cool, he had no weapon. It was unhandy to carry a firearm while working cattle.

Pearl still had her ever present pistol but had unbuckled it and hung it over her saddle horn. She ambled over to her horse and pulled it from the holster and held it close to her leg, the folds of her split riding skirt hiding it.

Mac Clem rode up to the fire and dismounted without being asked to. This was a blatant violation of etiquette. "Well, I see you're getting branded up Pearl. You don't need to do anymore, me and the boys will finish for you. You can send this scarecrow packing. He's just in the way now."

"I'll do as I please, Mac Clem, and sending my help away ain't going to happen. You stay off my range and we will get along just fine. I told you what would happen next time you came back, uninvited." Pearl drew a hard line.

"Well, you ain't got no shotgun today, so I'll just lay a few lumps on this scarecrow, and you and I can spend some time together." Mac started toward Whit.

Whit balled up his fist, ready to take on the bully, but before anyone could swing, Pearl jammed the pistol barrel into Mac's belly. "I told you I'd kill you, Mac."

With that, she pulled the trigger! The pistol didn't go off, looking down at it, the white faced Mac saw that the loose part of his shirt was stuck between the firing pin and the bullet. "Oh God, I think you meant to kill me!" He whispered.

"I told you I would. I've done it before and by God, I'll do it again." She thumbed the hammer back on the pistol to release the shirt, but before she could pull the trigger again, Whit had wrenched the gun away. "You don't want to do that. I'll take care of it." When Whit turned back to Mac, he smiled and said, "I think you need to move on. The lady asked nice."

"Like hell." But before Mac could finish his sentence Whit brought the running iron down around Mac's head, right below his ear.

Mac hit the ground like a pole-axed steer. Rolling to his hands and knees, he looked up. Whit still stood there with the iron, waiting to see what Mac would do next. Leaning forward just a little, he asked, "you are leaving now, aren't you?" Mac nodded, then slowly getting to his feet, wobbled to his horse. Looking back, through gritted teeth, he said, "this ain't done yet. I'll be back."

Whit smiled again. "I may not be able to stop her from shooting you next time. We got lots of old mine shafts to drop your carcass in. See ya."

Chapter 8

Finishing Up The Day

As Mac rode away. Whit found Pearl staring at him wide-eyed. "You wouldn't let me kill him, but you damn near caved his skull in. Give me back that pistol!"

"It ain't lady-like to shoot somebody, even somebody like Mac. He didn't need killing, just an attitude adjustment." Whit was grinning as he handed Pearl's pistol back to her. He put the running iron back in the fire to heat and added wood. "Let's get the cattle back up here. There's still some calves to brand."

Way up high, on the canyon wall, above the Kane Canyon Mine, was a rock overhang. Not really a cave, but a sheltered place out of the weather. The front had a wall of boulders that had fallen from above over the years. Behind those boulders sat Muchacho. He had a little fire going, coffee on, and was roasting a strip of meat. That morning, he had passed through the ranch headquarters. No one was home, so he had gone into the house and lifted a package of coffee, some salt and flour, and an old pot. Before he left, he had left four small gold nuggets on the table. Four was a sacred number to him. He was on foot, but there were no horses in the corral, so he walked on. Upon reaching the spring in Kane Canyon, he found a fat heifer calf. He brought her down with his bow, quietly. Butchering the calf, he wrapped the meat in the hide and climbed the canyon wall to the overhang. He was resting, waiting for the coffee to boil, when he heard the clink of a horseshoe below. Peering out from behind a boulder, he saw Mac riding slowly by, holding his head. Muchacho had decided to stay put for a few days and jerk the beef before heading back to the Sierra Madres. When younger, it wasn't unheard of for him to walk forty miles a day, no more. In his 64th year, he found he needed rest, more often. He had left the horses he had at San Carlos. He figured to steal or borrow one somewhere along the line, but had not come upon one yet. He had his rifle and an old pistol, also, his bow and a quiver full of arrows. He didn't plan on bringing attention to himself any more than he had to. Besides, he knew where those gold nuggets were in the mine below. They were worth nothing to him, but the white man put a lot of faith in the yellow iron. He would get a few more while he stayed secure in his hideout. He was going to rest.

Chapter 9

Morning

Whit was laying on his bunk, his hands behind his head. It was as hot as you could ever imagine. He had the door to the bunk room propped open and the window raised, trying to get a little breeze through. The air was heavy with humidity. It was one of those super-hot mornings that brought the thunderstorms out of Mexico. After a month of hard, daily riding and cow work, his every muscle was sore and every bone and joint ached, but he loved it. He didn't know how much weight he had gained, but his shirt was getting a little harder to button. He was filling out the seat of his britches and the persistent cough was about gone. One thing was nagging him. During the month of riding, they had branded more calves than pearl had thought she had cows for. They had found lots of unbranded young heifers and cows, many of them with baby calves already at their sides. But in all that riding they saw no young two or three-year-old bulls or steers. Did her cows only have heifer calves? The logical assumption was someone was harvesting her steer and bull cattle. But all the new bull calves were now branded with a heart with a (P) in the center on their ribs with the full crop earmarked. It would be a bit harder for a cinch ring artist to market them. Whit turned over on his bed. It was still two hours to daylight. He wanted a bit of sleep before he tackled the next day's chores.

Muchacho was squatting down behind a little stunted pine. Below him, a white man was looking out across the basin with a pair of binoculars. His gray horse was tied a few feet behind him. Muchacho had been watching this man for five days and knew he was spying on the man and woman in the basin. Raising his bow, he strung an arrow, a second later the twang of the bowstring was the last thing the white man heard. He rolled over in the rocks looking up at the black thunder clouds coming up from the south. Lightning flashed, but his eyes glazed over before he could see it. Muchacho walked up and began to strip the body. He was a treasure trove of things he needed. Loading all the things on the gray horse, he turned and rolled the now naked body into a crack in the rocks and filled it in with loose rock. This was one dead white man that disappeared in time with no explanation. Muchacho led the horse back down the canyon to the spring where the man had been camped and rummaged through the camp goods taking all the things that he might use. The rest he buried, as he had the body. After an hour, there was no evidence of a camp ever been there. The storm was growing closer. He wanted to be traveling while the coming rain was washing out his tracks. But first, he wanted to talk to the man in the basin, his friend.

Chapter 10

Confession

Whit and Pearl had just sat down to eat supper when the sound of a walking horse came from the yard. Pearl picked up her ever present pistol and stood to one side of the door.

Whit slowly got up from the table, shaking his head. He opened the door and saw a gray horse standing in the yard. From behind the horse stepped Muchacho. "Don't shoot." He said in Spanish. "I came to tell you good-bye. I'm going back to my home in the Sierra Madres. I will die there, I think. I wanted to tell you some things before the rain comes. For five days a man has been watching you and the Senora. I don't think he was a good man. I took his rifle, his pistol, his long eyes, and all the bullets and food. I took this horse and his scalp."

Whit was dumbfounded. "Long eyes?" He asked.

"He was using them to watch you." Muchacho held up the binoculars. No one will ever find him. But soon, a hard sheriff will come looking for him. You tell him I did this thing because you are my friend."

"Are you the Apache Kid?" Whit asked, not realizing the rudeness of the question.

"No, I am not. He died a long time ago, but many people think I am. I let them think it, it's easier that way. You can tell the nice Senora with the pistol; I will not harm you or her. You have been a friend. I have eaten your food, drank your coffee and you never thought bad of me or turned me away. I go now." Muchacho mounted the gray horse and as he turned him away, the brand became visible.

Pearl looked to Whit, "isn't that Mac's brand?" She asked in a whisper.

Whit solemnly nodded as they watched Muchacho ride off south into the approaching storm.

Chapter 11

Realization

Whit was laying in bed, a hot sweat soaked bed. The door was open to the yard letting in whatever breeze there might be. The big yellow moon hung overhead and illuminated the yard in a yellowish pale light. Whit had his hands behind his head and was staring out the door at Pearl's house over across the yard. A light flickered in a window. Whit thought to himself that Pearl was over there alone. Maybe snuggled down in her bed, lonesome. With a start Whit sat up. He suddenly realized he was going to be fine. The past few days, he had noticed his clothes a bit tighter. He had a harder time pulling his shirt together to button it. His pants had to be stretched a bit to button, and now he was actually thinking about that five foot two, robust woman over there. When he was mustered out of the army the doctors had told him he would never have carnal thoughts again. The fever had taken his ability for such things. Yet here he was wishfully thinking about that good woman over there. Was she as lonesome as he was? Did she yearn for a body laying close to her as he did? He swung his feet to the floor and started to stand up. But a sudden shiver hit him. The thought of that robust woman was clouded with the memory of that pistol under her pillow! He knew that wasn't a joke. He had seen Pearl try her best to shoot Mac Clem at close range and with no regret except she hadn't accomplished the task. Whit didn't think any of that was a bluff. Just as he started to lay back down with the realization that maybe he getting back to normal, with normal thoughts.

He heard the sound of a horse walking through the yard. Reaching next to the bed, he laid his hand on the Winchester he kept there. Pulling on his pants, he stepped bare footed to the door and peered out into the yard. A gray horse stood at the water trough. He had no saddle, bridle or rider. The animal held one front foot off the ground. Looking around carefully, he eased out the door and slipped over to the corral gate. He then eased around the horse and herded him into the corral. The horse was missing a lot of hair in places. A large lump had risen over the point of one shoulder. Hair was gone in scrapes off the hips and the root of his tailbone. Whit went into the barn and came back with a flake of hay.

Pearl stood at the fence in her nightgown, looking at the horse through the bars of the fence.

Whit laid the hay in front of the horse and stood up. "Isn't that the horse Muchacho rode away from here on?" Pearl asked.

"Yep, he's been in some sort of a wreck. "Whit was staring at Pearl whose hair was down and the moon was shining through the thin cotton nightgown.

"You think we ought to go hunt him up and see if he

is okay? I hate to think of any man laying out there hurt." Pearl was still looking at the horse.

"In the morning, I'll try and back track him. See if that ole Apache is still alive, and if he isn't, I'll give him a Christian burial." Whit turned and came out the gate.

"Okay, let's get to bed so we can get an early start." Upon saying that she had started to turn back to the house.

Whit had inadvertently started to follow her. "Your bed is in there Mister." She pointed to the barn.

Whit stopped in his tracks, not realizing he was following her.

"There may come a time you will sleep in my bed, but this isn't it yet. I have to think on you for a bit more." Pearl spoke low and smiled when she spoke.

Whit nodded and turned to his own room. Well, there it was, he was getting better, within himself and with Pearl.

Chapter 12

The Search

The next morning, Pearl and Whit left the ranch a short hour before dawn. There was just enough light to make out the tracks, left by Muchacho's gray horse. Traveling at a ground covering jog trot, they were sure that the trail was going into Kane Canyon. They traveled down to the river, then south, back to Mexico. As they approached the mouth of the canyon, the tracks turned south along the east face of the Dripping Springs Mountains.

Whit pulled up, dismounted and walked along, leading his horse, and bent over the tracks as if to see better. As they rounded a house sized boulder, a wide trail opened up before them, an old and wide trail. It continued south, but was gradually climbing in elevation. Remounting when he was sure of the tracks before him, Whit started on, Pearl followed, leading a spare horse. If they found the old Apache, they wanted to be able to take him home.

The trail wound and twisted among some of the roughest country Whit had ever seen, all the while it slowly climbed gave a clear view of the country below. By midafternoon, the trail had narrowed and became rougher and harder to see. The ground was loose and many times their horses would step and slide a foot or two downhill. The going was slow, to say the least. Then the trail turned down a sharp canyon; not as large as Kane Canyon, but the walls were just as steep and rocky.

As they reached the boulder strewn floor, there was a spot where the ground had been torn up. The imprint of a horse's hoof was clearly outlined in the soft sand. To one side lay a saddle and bridle, a couple of morales, empty, laying under a scrub mesquite. Looking around, Pearl found a horseshoe, bent and twisted, with a piece of hoof wall still held in place by the horseshoe nails. Muchacho's horse had overreached, catching the front shoe and fell.

Riding in a short circle, Pearl found signs that someone had been dragging something into the rocks. She called to Whit. Seeing the drag marks, Whit dismounted and softly called to Muchacho in Spanish. No answer came. Motioning to Pearl to stay put, he handed her his bridle reins. He started following the drag trail. After rounding a boulder the size of a small house, he called again.

To his left, in a tumble of gray boulders, came a feeble voice. "Over here White Man. I won't shoot." In the shade of a boulder lay the Apache. He was stretched out, his legs at an odd angle. His head was propped up on a small rock. His rifle lay next to him, a long dead fire, cold ashes a few feet away. A morale lay close, but no water was in sight. "Do you have water White Man?" The Indian asked.

Turning, Whit called to Pearl to bring the canteen. That his legs were broken was obvious, but something else was wrong. Whit could see that Muchacho held himself ridged. "Where does it pain you old friend?"

"Inside, I think something broken. If I move very much, I can't breathe and I spit blood. I die soon, I think." The old man spoke through gritted teeth. After a few sips of water, Muchacho seemed a bit relaxed. He reached over for his morale. Whit took hold of it to hand it to the Indian. It was surprisingly heavy. Looking inside, it was full of jerky, but it was much heavier than just jerky. He looked toward the old Apache with an unasked question. Whit pulled the morale closer. "It's for the good woman." He pointed to Pearl. "She will need it soon for her rancho. The big man will come again soon." With that, Muchacho drifted off to sleep.

Pearl opened the bag and peered inside. "It's just jerky, how is that a help? I guess I won't go hungry when Mac shows up."

Whit dug in the bag, down to the bottom. His hand came back out, clutching a fist full of shining gold nuggets. "I don't think you will go hungry."

Pearl's eyes were big with surprise. She looked at Muchacho and found him staring at her. He nodded and whispered, "In the canyon." Then he closed his eyes and breathed his last breath, far from his home in the Sierra Madres.

They had found a crack in the rocks, wrapped the old Apache in a blanket and lay him in it, in the Apache way. They then carried rocks, filling in the crack, leaving the body there. After a few moments, they had mounted and started home in the gathering darkness. A long sad ride home.

By a sliver of moon overhead, Whit and Pearl rode into the ranch yard. Slung from her saddle horn was Muchachos morale.

Chapter 13

After The Storm

Whit was standing in the kitchen doorway with a cup of coffee. The rain had left a fresh clean world, devoid of dust and tracks. He raised his cup, when in the distance he could see three men coming up out of the canyon and long trotting across the basin toward the ranch house.

He turned and spoke to Pearl, who was clearing the table. "Men coming, maybe old Muchacho was a good fortune teller."

Pearl stepped in behind Whit and looked over his shoulder at the approaching riders. "Mmmmm, seems old Mac went for help."

Whit nodded and turned to the stove to refill his cup. "Well, we will see what their story is. Keep that pistol in the holster and your temper intact." He grinned at her.

A few minutes later, the riders long trotted into the yard and pulled up in front of the house. Whit still leaned against the doorjamb, his cup in his hand. "I'm Sheriff Jackson, I'm looking for Pearl Heart." The man in the middle spoke. He was of medium size with a full stomach, straining his shirt buttons.

Pearl stepped out onto the porch. "What can I do for

you?" She asked.

"I have a warrant for your arrest on the charge of attempted murder. Hand over that pistol and let's go. Is this scarecrow your hired man?"

Before she could answer, Mac Clem pushed his horse forward. "That's him Sheriff. I don't know his name, but that's the man who assaulted me." Mac was rubbing the welt under his ear.

"Well, I got a warrant for a John Doe, so I guess you're my pigeon." The sheriff smiled a broken toothed smile.

"Where you from Sheriff? I don't believe I've seen you around." Pearl stepped forward, her hand resting on her hip.

"I'm out of Florence, Pinal County, now come along." He replied.

"Well, this is Gila County and you have no jurisdiction. You take those warrants to Globe and give them to the deputy there. He will serve them. If you're taking Mac Clem's word for anything, get ready to get embarrassed. I sure did try to shoot him. He was going to assault me and my man here. He admitted to beating up my two former hired men, so they would leave, and if you're gonna insist on serving those warrants, I'll press charges on Mac Clem for cattle theft. We will see how far any of this goes. Now there's the road to Globe. Take it if you want. I'll surrender to the deputy from Gila County, but not to a two by twice Pinal deputy." While Pearl was talking, Whit had reached inside the house and laid his hand on Pearl's shotgun. "We don't want any trouble Sheriff, but like Pearl said, you got no jurisdiction here, and as for Mr. Clem there, he has had a man spying on us for at least five days, watching us work. For what reason, I can only speculate as to why. An Apache killed him and took his horse. He told us that, so go chase him if you want. If not, just go chase your tail."

Clem started backing his horse away, his face bleached white. The sheriff turned to him, "is all that true? You didn't tell me any of this. I won't touch them without a Gila County Deputy, but I think these warrants just might get lost in the shuffle. You've been running loose too long yourself." Clem turned his horse and spurred out of the yard, looking back over his shoulder as he went.

"Well there's your answer Sheriff. We will be right here when ya get back with the Gila County law." Pearl leaned a bit forward when she spoke.

"I'm not going to Globe yet. I want to see what my County Attorney says first." He turned his horse, and with his deputy following, struck a trot toward Kane Canyon.

Mac Clem was already out of sight, raising dust back down the canyon.

Chapter 14

Commitment

The next morning, while it was later than usual, Pearl was cooking a steak and egg breakfast. Biscuits were in the oven and outside, the sun was up and Whit was doing chores. They had ridden through the night, getting home after midnight. They, as well as their horses, were done in. Pearl was still unable to sleep. She had too much on her mind, the gold nuggets, Whit, the ranch, all were unanswered questions. Out there somewhere, Mac Clem was still an issue. She stepped to the kitchen door and rang the bell that hung on the porch beam, calling Whit to breakfast.

When Whit came in the door, Pearl had set a plate of steak and eggs with fried potatoes on the table in his usual place. She slid a plate full of fresh hot biscuits toward him, a dish with butter followed. She poured two cups of coffee while he dug into the food and set them on the table. Buttering a biscuit for herself, she sat down opposite of Whit. While he ate, she absent-mindedly chewed the biscuit and sipped coffee. As he was wiping the last of the egg-yoke from his plate with a biscuit, Pearl looked him in the eye. "Do you love me?" She asked.

The question hit him right between the eyes. He sat back and looked at her with a scared, but determined, stare. After a moment, he answered, "I don't know what it is to love someone. I need you, not just for the food and the job, but for your friendship. You're important to me. I respect you, and I want your respect. When I came here, I wasn't far from being dead. I was ready for it. You had no reason to do the things you've done for me. In that respect, I owe you. But does all that add up to love? I don't know. The only love I ever knew was fifteen minutes in a crib with a two-dollar chippy. Good love? Honest love? I don't know. Why would a good-looking woman ask me, probably the homeliest man around, if I love her? You could do so much better than me."

"Whit, I asked you that because I feel something for you. It's more than friendship, although there's that too. I've had handsome men, and not one was worth a busted nickel-plated watch. Yes, I fed you, you were hungry, and yes, you have worked like an African fieldhand to pay for the meals. You have stuck your neck out for me when you could have ridden on. I think your heart is good and pure, no matter what has transpired in the past. That's worth more than anything to me. You overlooked my past, never a mention of it, and I've tried to respect you the same way. Let's face it, we aren't getting any younger and the thought of getting old alone scares me. Do you understand what I'm saying? With all that said, I think that adds up to love. You're loyal, honest, and true. No man was ever that way with me before."

Whit got up and went to the stove and filled his cup,

then filled Pearl's. "Then I guess I love you. I know I sure need you. But I have nothing to put into this deal, but my two bare hands. Hell, I can hardly drive a nail in a board. What have I got to bring into this? A worn out saddle and horse? You could do much better than me. You're a very attractive woman. Past or no past, I would be the luckiest man around to have you for my woman."

Pearl got up from the table, walked to Whit, pressed her body against his, and kissed him long and passionately. When she backed away a step, she looked him in the eye and said, "there, that seals the deal."

Whit, trying to catch his breath and reeling from the wave of emotion stammered, "well I guess it does." He set his cup on the drainboard and backed to the door. "I, uh, got some things to do, I'll, uh be uh right outside." He smiled his crooked smile. He turned to go out the door. The door jamb next to his face exploded, sending a shower of wood splinters into his face, then he heard a distant boom from outside. Whit staggered back into the kitchen and fell to a sitting position by the table. Another shot sounded as a bullet screamed through the kitchen. Pearl was kneeling by Whit, the side of his face looked like a nest of porcupine quills, he was in shock. He reached up to touch his cheek and Pearl pulled his hand down. He said, "that was one hell of a kiss Pearl Heart."

Pearl slid over to the open door and pushed it shut with her foot. "Damn Mac Clem, I'll kill him yet." She slid back over to Whit. Reaching up to the table, she retrieved her pistol belt. "I'll kill him, I'll kill him if it's the last thing I do."

Chapter 15

Battle

Pearl checked the loads in her pistol.

Whit lay back on the floor. "I feel like my face is on fire." He again reached up to it, but Pearl stopped him, pulling his hand down and whispering in his ear. "Lay still, he's still out there. Don't move."

A shadow crossed the kitchen window, a step on the porch outside the door, the doorknob started to slowly turn.

Pearl thumbed back the hammer on the pistol. "I'll kill you Mac," she whispered under her breath.

As the door slowly opened, a rifle barrel came through the gap. It pushed the door open and a tall man stepped in only to see Pearl sitting on the floor next to a man with a face full of splinters. The pistol exploded in her hand and he reeled back, starting to fall. The pistol banged twice more in quick succession. The man lay half in and half out the door. The rifle at his side. Without a backward glance, Pearl turned to Whit. Droplets of blood were showing through the splinters. Getting up, she went to the stove and got a pan of hot water and a towel. Helping Whit to his feet, she sat him in a kitchen chair.

His eyes had a distant look. "Damn this burns," was

all he said.

"I got nothing for the pain. This is gonna hurt, but I need to pull that wood out of your cheek. I can't kiss a man with that much wood stuck in his face." She smiled a grim smile.

"Well, give her hell Lady. I don't want to miss any more kisses." Whit slid a chair over and gripped the back of it with both hands.

Pearl started pulling the splinters from Whit's face. Not even a whimper came from him, but he turned a pasty color, and his hands trembled as they gripped the chair. The long ones she pulled by hand, the small slivery ones she used tweezers. When done, she wet a towel and pressed it to his face. A sigh emitted from his lips. Getting up, Pearl went to the carcass laying on her doorstep. "Damn, that's not Mac Clem," she exclaimed. The man lay on his side. She toed him over onto his back, a white piece of folded paper showed in his vest pocket. She pulled it out, it was a handbill, promising 500 dollars to whoever killed Whit. Payment to be made at the Battle Axe Ranch from Mac Clem. "I'll kill the son of a bitch!" Pearl almost screamed, her hands shaking with anger.

Whit had gotten up and staggered over and was staring at the corpse. The first bullet had gone through the man, under his armpit on the left side, through his heart and out the right side. The next two had gone through his neck and temple as he was falling from the first. Anyone of the three shots would have killed him. Holding the towel next to his cheek Whit mumbled, "damn, I hope you never get mad at me."

Pearl and Whit dragged the corpse out on the porch and covered it with a piece of tarp. "Over at the mining town of Troy there's a wire. It's only eight or ten miles. I'll go see if I can send a wire for the law. You keep that towel on your face and a gun handy. I'll be back soon." Pearl stepped down off the porch and headed to the barn.

Whit watched her stride off, a sway to her hips making her riding skirt swing from side to side. "Hell of a kiss," he mumbled.

Chapter 16

Aftermath

Whit was riding out, checking the cattle. It had been two weeks since the shooting at Pearl's house. His face was healing, even though it was a bit pock marked from the splinters. After Pearl had wired for the deputy sheriff, he had arrived the next day. He spent enough time to get a statement from them both and helped bury the corpse. He had no idea as to the identity of the shooter. He had nothing on him, but in his pocket were eight rifle cartridges. His horse was tied back behind the barn and held nothing to identify the man. After burying the corpse, the deputy had taken the horse and saddle with him when he left, saying he was confiscating them for the county. As he rode away, Pearl had mumbled, "like hell. He's confiscating them for himself."

"That's okay. I confiscated the rifle." Whit had chuckled. Whit had been out since daylight and was covering a lot of ground, looking at a lot of cattle. It hadn't rained in a while and the grass was brown and dried. The cattle were holding up, but Whit knew it was just a matter of time before they started losing weight, especially the cows with calves sucking. Up ahead was a water hole with some small cottonwood and hackberry trees around it. He decided it would be a good place to rest a bit and maybe eat his lunch. As he rode up, he could smell something dead. Riding over the bank, in the hole there before him was a bloated carcass of a bull laying in the hole, stuck in the drying mud. The spring that normally fed this hole had dried up and nothing remained, but mud and the bull. Dropping his rope on the dead animal's head, he tugged the carcass out of the mud and dragged it away from the hole. Retrieving his rope, he rode around to the back side under a cottonwood tree and stepped down and loosened the cinches on the sorrel horse. Digging in his saddle pocket, he found the sandwich Pearl had made for him and settled down in the shade to eat. He knew if the breeze shifted, the smell from the bull might run him out from under this tree, but until then, he was settled in. Looking out across the flat toward the ranch house, he could just make out a rider coming at a jog. Speaking to no one in particular, Whit said, "well here comes the boss to check on me. "He wiggled down in the sand and settled back until she got there.

As Pearl rode up, a smile was on her pretty face, "why you lazy bum, sleeping on the job."

"Nope, saw ya comin'. figured I better stay put and report," Whit deadpanned. He then explained the spring being dry and the dead bull stuck in the mud. "I suppose you wanna take that outta my wages?" He cinched up his horse and they rode away together to check another water hole. Maybe things were worse than they thought.

Chapter 17

Worry

The west end of the barn had a sliver of shade from the eave of the roof. In this shade, Whit had an upturned wooden keg, he used for a seat. He was sitting there staring out across the landscape of dry, dusty pasture land. Heatwaves danced and floated during the midafternoon heat. In his left hand, he held the four little gold nuggets that Muchacho had left him. He wallowed them about in his palm, rubbed them together, and continued to absent mindedly play with them.

Quietly and softly, Pearl stepped out of the barn and sat down next to him on the ground, her back against the barn wall. "What are you looking at Whit man?"

"Nothing in particular. Just trying to figure out how to keep this cow outfit in drinking water." He didn't look up from his stare. "The tanks are dry; the springs are down to a trickle and aren't keeping up. If it doesn't rain soon, you're going to find more than that bull dead. Might think about selling out or maybe drive this herd down to the river."

Pearl's soft eyes grew big and hard, "down to the river? That's the Battle Axe, that's Mac Clem's outfit. Why don't we just invite him up here to help himself?" She was adamant.

"Well, it's going to come to that or watch them die.

There's no water. Unless you know where there's a magical source, bubbling from the ground." Whit was getting mad.

Pearl leaned back against the wall again. "Well, I just might know of such a place. I'll be damned if I'll help Mac help himself to more of my cows."

"If you know of such a place, you better speak up, or you're gonna have a mess on your hands." Whit was serious.

"I'll take you there in the morning. We will make a picnic out of it." Pearl was winking at him. She brushed the dirt off her butt as she walked away, back to the house.

"Picnic! damn, this ain't no pink tea party!" Whit was mumbling to himself as he got to his feet.

Chapter 18

Water

Pearl snapped the lines down the backs of the team of Cleveland Bays that were hitched to her Studebaker buckboard. Whit sat next to her, holding on to the seat handles. In the back was a wicker basket with their picnic lunch and a shovel and pick. The bay team struck a long jerking trot over the rocky trail that led down to Kane Canyon. Just before entering the canyon, a faint track turned off to the north and Pearl pulled the team down to a flat-footed walk and turned onto the trail. She had one booted foot up against the dashboard while Whit was trying to keep his seat on the rough ride. The two-track was overgrown with grass and weeds, so Pearl kept the team to a walk. It was still rough as the wheels rolled over protruding rocks and brush.

Far ahead, Whit could make out a tendril of smoke rising. "What's that?" He asked, pointing at the column rising in the distance.

"That's Troy, about a hundred people live there, we aren't going that far." Pearl spoke through gritted teeth as the wagon bounced over another rock. A mile further on, they came to the edge of a deep draw. The track stopped at the edge of a rocky drop off. Down below, Whit could make out the ruins of a rock cabin, an arrastra, and a head frame over a square shaft. Tying the team to a handy cedar tree, Pearl grabbed the basket and told Whit to get the shovel and pick. She then started down an old worn footpath. Upon reaching the bottom, she went over to the cabin next to a wall in the shade and set the basket down.

Whit came stumbling along, but stopped when he was next to the square shaft. He could hear water rushing down below. "What the hell?" He asked.

"A miner over in Troy told me about it. He and a friend were working on this claim when they hit the underground stream. They couldn't bail it fast enough and abandoned it. He told me I could take all the water we needed as long as he could work the claim if it ever went dry." Pearl was smiling like a poker player with four aces.

The shaft was on a bench in the canyon bottom, about forty feet up from the floor. Looking down the side of the mountain, you could see the canyon fed into a large earthen dam and stock tank. "All we gotta do is get that water running down the wash to the tank down there, shouldn't be too hard." Pearl was grinning at Whit.

"How are we supposed to do that, with a pick and shovel? You're off your rocker Girl." Whit was shaking his head.

"Look, the water is just fifteen feet down the shaft, all we gotta do is cut into it below that and we have a free-flowing stream." Pearl was walking back to the basket.

"That's thirty feet of rock to dig through. I'll be two weeks, cutting in there." Whit was flabbergasted.

"No, just dig a good sized hole along the way we want the water to go, then we use this." She held up a bundle of giant powder sticks she had taken from the basket.

"Holy cow, Woman, we had that bouncing over all the rocks? We could've been blown to bits." Whit snatched the bundle from pearl.

"No, I had the caps here in my shirt pocket, we were safe as a baby in a carriage." Pearl held out five blasting caps in her palm.

"Jesus Woman." Was all Whit said, as he turned to the shaft. Picking a good slope, then using the pick, he started breaking the ground as close to the shaft as he could. While he swung the pick, Pearl laid out the lunch whistling a gay tune. After a two hour stint with the pick and shovel, Whit came up to where Pearl had lunch ready and plopped down next to her smiling. "I think you're on to something Lady." He bit into a deviled egg.

Pearl poured him a glass of lemonade and he leaned back against the rock wall munching his meal. Later, Pearl took the basket and climbed the canyon wall to the team. Untying them, she turned and drove them back away from the canyon. Down in the canyon, Whit had placed the dynamite as close to the shaft wall as he could. He had spotted the fuses and caps using a good twenty feet of slow fuse. Packing loose dirt around the bundle, he then struck a match, lit the fuse, and ran up the trail to the top of the rim, as he reached it a horrific blast shook the earth, and dirt, rocks, and mud rained down around him. Getting back to his feet, he looked down at the bottom of the canyon. A stream of muddy water, a foot deep and three feet across, was starting to rush down the stream bed. "I told you it would work." Pearl had walked up behind Whit and laid her hand on his shoulder.

"Let's hope it holds, there haven't been any cattle over here in a while. We could move all of yours here, if the water is strong enough." Whit hugged her. "Let's start home. We will check tomorrow to see how much hits the dam down below."

A few minutes later, the team was headed home, with Whit holding the reins.

Pearl snuggled up next to him, a smile on her pretty face.

Chapter 19

Relocating

Before sun up the next morning, Whit had a good bay horse between his legs and was long trotting toward the Troy tank to see how much water it had caught. By cutting cross country, he was able to reach the tank in a long hour. As he rode up to the dam side of the tank, a large covey of quail and two buck deer left out to one side. Whit knew there was some water or the wildlife wouldn't be there. As he topped the dam, a large pond of water greeted him. Mud hens swam about contentedly and a few cows and calves were laying in the shade of the mesquites on one side of the pond. Overnight, it had become an oasis. Circling to the upper end, he saw that if anything, the stream of water had increased. He was amazed at the amount coming down the wash. Riding upstream toward the mine, he could see sparkling flakes of mineral in the stream of clear water. Shaking his head, he still couldn't believe that this existed during a bad drought. Upon reaching the mine shaft, he could see that overnight the water had washed the wall of the shaft deeper, allowing more of the water to flow down the wash. The shaft wall had washed out below the crack that had allowed the water to keep running underground. Now the channel that fed the shaft was visible and it was incredible, the stream that flowed from it. Whit turned his horse up the foot trail to the top of the bank. Gaining the higher elevation, he could look back down country toward the ranch house. A speck was moving in his direction with a group of other specks in front. Pearl was bringing some cattle to the tank.

Smiling to himself, Whit turned his horse to go help when he came face to face with a man sitting on a horse. He wore bib overalls and brogan shoes with a soft cap perched on a dirty head. His greasy hair sticking out from beneath the sweatband. "My name is Riely, who are you?" He asked.

"They call me Whit. I work for Pearl Boot." Whit tried not to act surprised.

"You mean you work for Pearl Hart, the woman bandit, don't you?" The man had a belligerent sneer on his face.

"I believe she is not a bandit anymore. Yes, that's her. We are moving some cattle here today." Whit tried to be friendly.

"Yeah, well, I work over at Troy. We heard an explosion yesterday over this way, so I came to check it out. You the one who blew up the shaft over there?" Riely had a grouch on.

"Yes, Pearl had permission from the claim owner. This will help him and us. Pearl is coming down below with some cattle. You can talk to her about it." Now Whit was getting edgy.

"No, I don't need to. Just don't be trying to mine

anything here. It's all part of the Troy district. We heard all about you two from an honest rancher." Riely was still being aggressive.

"And just who would that be?" Whit asked.

"Mac Clem, he's been staying over with us the last few days. You know him?" Riely leaned a bit forward as though he was throwing Clem's name at Whit.

"Yes I know him, and the status of his honesty is still in question. Be careful you don't harbor a varmint. The sheriff from Globe has a warrant for him, as does the one from Florence. But you do as you wish." Whit threw the accusation right back at Riely.

Riely jerked his horse around and thumped him in the ribs with his bare heels and trotted down the footpath and headed back to Troy.

Shaking his head, Whit turned to see Pearl was having trouble with her bunch of cattle. They were spreading out, trying to turn back. He loped off down the country to help her. He could see a week's worth of work ahead, bringing the cattle back into this forgotten corner of the ranch.

Chapter 20

Watchful

The next few days were long and hard. Whit and Pearl, before daylight, were horseback moving cattle to the Troy part of the ranch. The water continued to run from the blasted mine shaft. Whit kept a close eye on the stream, waiting for it to run dry, but the flow was strong. The Troy tank was full and water was starting to dribble over the spillway. Many of the cattle, once they got a good drink, insisted on returning to their home pasture. But Pearl and Whit kept after them to relocate to the fresh feed and water. One thing Whit noticed was Pearl, upon hearing that Mac Clem was seen in the town of Troy had started wearing the six-gun on her hip again. Even when cooking a meal back at the house, she wore it. When Whit mentioned it, she quietly told him she wasn't taking any chances with Mac showing up at an unsuspected time. They had seen no one in their work, but Whit had seen strange horse tracks at various places. He said nothing to Pearl, but kept a wary eye out. Then came a morning when Whit, while moving a handful of cattle to the Troy tank, rode up on a yearling heifer that had been butchered. Those strange horse tracks were there. Only a hind quarter had been taken and the rest of the meat was left to the scavengers. Growling his anger, Whit started following the horse tracks, leaving the butchered animal. After a mile, the tracks became more distinct and proved to be the same ones Whit had been seeing. They were heading in a bee-line for Troy. Between him and Troy, Whit could make out a rider. He rode to a rise and watched the rider as he rode into the back of the buildings of Troy. That was enough for Whit. He turned his horse for the ranch. He would get a deputy before he went into Troy. He knew it would take some kind of convincing to keep Pearl and her ever present six-shooter from storming the miners' homes.

Chapter 21

Ranger

Whit shoved the scared old Winchester down in the saddle holster and tied it in place. He then untied the pack horse who had been tied to the fence and mounted his saddle horse. With Pearl gone to Globe for the law, Whit figured to camp at the artesian water until they returned. In the west, storm clouds were building and flashes of lightning could be seen under them. He thought to himself, *if it rains it might wash all their troubles away.* Smiling to himself, he tugged on the lead rope and headed up country. Pearl long trotted her give out horse down the street into Globe. She had left the ranch before daylight and rode hard all the way there. The sorrel was done in, nothing left. She had to ride around a Maxwell touring car parked in the street. Its front wooden spoked wheels turned into the curb to keep it from rolling down the hill.

Stepping down from the jaded horse, she didn't even bother to tie him, just dropped the reins and hurried into the sheriff's office. The sweat ran down the horse's legs and made puddles around his feet. His head hung down between his front legs. Stepping into the office, the deputy was behind his desk doing paperwork. In the corner, a long lean man sat in a straight-back chair reading a newspaper.

"What ya need Pearl?" The deputy asked looking up from his work. His tone changed a bit when he realized the mood Pearl was in.

"I've had a beef butchered by someone over to Troy. I need you to come out and get the varmint." Pearl was dead serious, with a demanding tone in her voice.

"Now, Pearl, I can't ride all the way out there over a butchered beef, and besides....." he didn't get to finish.

"Well, how bout serving that warrant on Mac Clem? You can do that can't you? One of them miners told me he was staying over there."

When Pearl said Mac Clem, the man in the corner rustled his paper while folding it as he stood. "You know where he is?" He asked as he walked over.

"I just said he was over to Troy. Who are you?" Pearl turned to the man.

"Dean Ellison, Arizona Ranger. I'll go back with you. We want him for some other things. I've got lots of paper on him. When can you go?" The tall man leaned down just a bit to speak to Pearl.

"As soon as I get a fresh horse. Mine is done in, if he hasn't fallen over dead in the street." She whirled to go out the door. Gathering up the reins, she started to lead the horse toward a livery across the street. Looking back at the ranger, she said, "I'll get a fresh mount and be right there."

Ellison stepped down off the walk and hollered. "You don't need a horse, just your saddle and gear."

Stripping the saddle from the sweaty animal, Pearl looked out the barn door in time to see a Ford Model T roll up outside. She had never ridden in one, but figured it was a fast way home. Loading her saddle in the back, shifting her pistol to her hip, she jumped in and the rig left with a lurch and a cloud of dust.

Turning to Pearl, Ellison said, "this will save time and horseflesh. I hope you have extra horses at the ranch?"

Pearl simply nodded. While she had both feet planted and braced against the floorboards, she was holding on to the door frame overhead with one hand and her hat with the other. The road was rocky and rutted from wagon travel. Ellison kept both hands on the wheel, twisting it and turning around the rocks and the bumps. A sneer was pasted to his face like he was in hand to hand combat with a slick Apache warrior. The dust rolled up behind them as they roared down the road. The dark clouds in the west were closer and the air had a heavy feel. Pearl wondered how this machine would do in the mud or if it was lightning proof. Pearl mentioned her concerns to the ranger, but either he didn't hear the question or didn't know the answer. In any case, he was frozen to the wheel like death on a grim African field hand. Pearl prayed for the first time in years.

Chapter 22

Closing The Gate

The rain and thunder had moved on down the side of the mountain, headed east. Whit had moved his bed and camp into a corner of the old rock house where a piece of the roof still protected things. A trickle of rain runoff was slipping by in the channel below the cabin. Whit walked outside in the dark and stirred the coals on his cook fire. He found the embers still hot, so he placed some dry wood from the nearby pile on it and watched as the flames slowly took hold. While the fire was popping and sizzling, he opened a can of peaches and sat on a nearby rock and started spearing slices out of the can with his pocketknife.

Into the circle of light rode Pearl and Ellison, their slickers glistening with rainwater. Pearl's old felt hat had melted down around her ears. She slipped from the wet saddle and leaned against the horse's shoulder.

Whit turned the peach can up and slurped the last of the juice, then threw the empty can off to one side as he went to her.

She looked up at him and tried to smile. "I didn't expect you until tomorrow. Had the throttle pulled way back coming this late." Whit hugged her.

"His fault," she grinned, pointing to Ellison. "He's an Arizona Ranger, has some paper on Mac, and is in a hurry to get him."

Ellison was uncinching his horse and pulling the gear from the steaming back. "Where can I catch some sleep?" He asked as he dumped his gear against the rock wall of the arrastra.

"Oh, anywhere you can find an empty spot, mi casa su casa." Whit thought he was funny. But Ellison only stared at him, pulled a doubled Navajo blanket out from under his saddle, and rolled up in it against the arrastra.

Whit took Pearl into the stone cabin. His bedroll was spread in a dry corner. "Get to bed, you're beat. I'll take care of the horses." He turned to go, but Pearl grabbed him and hugged him again. "I'm glad you're okay. You are coming back, right?" She pleaded.

"Just leave me room, I'll be back quick." He gave her a peck on the cheek. The next morning, Whit had the coffee pot gurgling and was slicing bacon into the skillet. A dutch-oven sat at one side with coals mounded high baking biscuits.

Ellison was at one side saddling his horse. "Since you been here, you haven't seen Mac?" He asked.

"Haven't seen a soul since I been here. But I can see Troy pretty well from here and I haven't seen anyone leave or go there, for that matter. If you will wait until this food is done, I'll go over there with you. You might need some backup." Whit was pouring a cup of coffee as he spoke.

Accepting the coffee. Ellison shook his head. "No, I wouldn't want anyone else involved. If you got hurt, that nice little woman in there might come after me with her pistol. It's my job, I'll tend to it."

Whit nodded and pulled a biscuit from the dutch-oven and put a couple of slices of bacon on it, he handed it to Ellison. "Have it your way, but he's a cowardly son, don't trust him to stand up in front of you."

Ellison threw the dregs from the coffee cup to one side and stuffed the rest of the biscuit in his mouth. Rolling it over to one side as he stepped up on the horse, he said, "Thanks I'll keep that in mind. Watch for us, I hope to be back by noon." With that, he spun the horse and headed up the trail toward Troy.

Mac Clem had had enough of Troy. The rainstorm had whipped the greasy tent he stayed in to rags and he was hungry most of the time. As were the miners. There was no booze allowed in camp, no gambling, and no whores. It wasn't what he wanted in a hangout. He was going back to his Battle Ax Ranch and then maybe get out of the country. Warrants with his name on them in two counties wasn't a good thing. He had a little cash put away at the ranch, plus some of the cattle he had mavericked from Pearl, he would head for Denver or maybe California. He was riding along thinking about his new plans, when coming toward him he saw a tall man on a bay horse. Mac ducked into a mesquite thicket out of sight and let the rider go past without seeing him. He didn't know why, but he had an uneasy feeling about this man.

At camp, Pearl was squatted down by the fire washing the last of the dishes. Whit had taken the horses to a fresh piece of ground to graze. She was humming a little tune under her breath when a big hand grabbed a hand full of her hair and jerked her to her feet. Trying to turn around, she realized that Mac Clem was grinning at her. She reached for her pistol, he deftly snaked it from her holster and tossed it aside. "No, you don't Darlin'. You don't need that." Mac said with a snarl. "It's been a while comin' but I'm sure this is gonna be well worth the wait." He slowly twisted her around to face him. Her toes just barely touching the ground. She spit in his face and tried to scratch his eyes with her fingernails, he simply leaned back and laughed.

From behind him, Mac heard a metallic click. "Put her down Scum. I'm fresh loaded." Whit stood by the arrastra wall, the Winchester held alongside his hip, pointed at Mac.

Mac froze for a second, then looked back over his shoulder at Whit. "Hell, it's only the lunger." He said to Pearl, who was squirming and kicking. Mac turned around, holding Pearl in front of him. He started backing toward his horse, pulling her along. As he reached the horse, he grinned at Whit "I'll just take this with me to be sure you don't back shoot me, Lunger."

"I'll shoot your front, back, any way you want. Put

her down and I won't shoot." Whit had moved a step closer.

"Naw, I don't trust you Lunger, besides I don't think you could hit the side of the mountain with that ole gosh danger." Keeping his hold on Pearl's hair, he stepped up on the horse.

Pearl through gritted teeth, looked at Whit. "Kill this son of a bitch Whit, kill him, never mind me, kill him."

Mac jerked her up in front of him and whirled the horse to leave, when Pearl still fighting and struggling, leaned to one side. At that moment, the Winchester barked. Blood spouted from Mac Clem's back. His grip on Pearl loosened and she fell, while he spurred his horse for the last time. Mac clung to the saddle horn for three strides of the horse when the scarred old Winchester roared again, sweeping him from the saddle. He bounced on the ground like a ball of rags and lay still.

Pearl got up, walked over to the dead man, spit on him, and kicked him in the face. "Well, I guess that finished him off for sure."

The voice came from above on the trail. Ellison was sitting on his horse.

Whit was sitting on the stone wall of the arrastra with the rifle leaning against one knee. His hands were shaking. His head hung low. Ellison rode up, stepped down, and asked if he was all right. "I'm good, just never shot anyone before. But he could have hurt Pearl."

Whit's color had become very pale.

Pearl came and sat next to him and put her arm around him. "Thanks, Whit. You were there again when I needed you."

Ellison had loaded the carcass on his horse and tied him down. "I'll leave your horse at the ranch Pearl. Thanks for the loan. Come to Globe when you can to fill out the report. I'll hang around and wait for you."

Pearl nodded as Ellison rode away toward the ranch. Whit looked at Pearl and opened his clenched fist, in it was four little smooth gold nuggets. "I guess old Muchacho left them for good luck. They came in handy."

Pearl sniffled.

"These aren't the ones he left, look at this arrastra floor." Whit was pointing to it. The cracks in the stone floor were packed with small nuggets of the fine gold. "I just raked a few out just now. Let's load up and head to town with them. There might be enough for me to buy half interest in a ranch. Ya think?"

www.ingramcontent.com/pod-product-compliance
Lightning Source LLC
Chambersburg PA
CBHW061711130726

47996CB00006B/2252